もうすぐ結婚する女

松田 青子

Aoko Matsuda

Translated by Angus Turvill

the girl who is getting married

strangers press

UEA PUBLISHING PROJECT
NORWICH

The Girl Who Is Getting Married
Aoko Matsuda

Translated from the Japanese by
Angus Turvill

First published by
Strangers Press, Norwich, 2017
part of UEA Publishing Project

Distributed by
NBN International

Printed by
Swallowtail Print, Norwich

Series editors
David Karashima
Elmer Luke

Editorial team
Kate Griffin
Nathan Hamilton
Philip Langeskov

Cover design and typesetting
Nigel Aono–Billson
Glen Robinson

Illustration and Design © 2017, Nigel Aono-Billson

ISBN-13: 978-1911343059

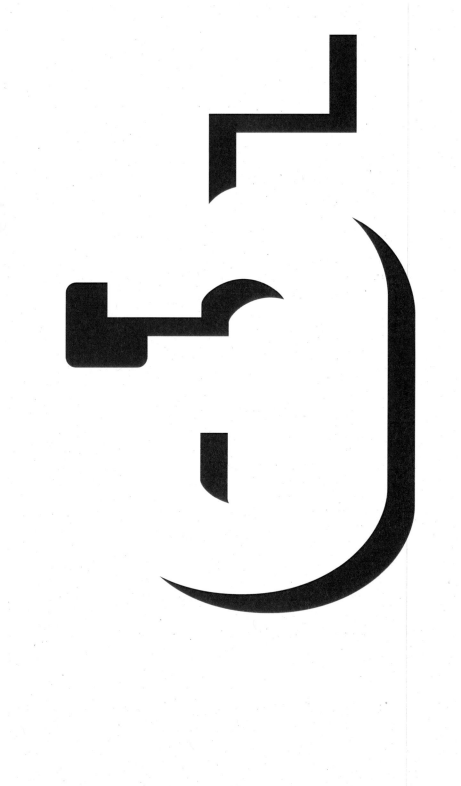

Foreword

The first sentence of Aoko Matsuda's seemingly lighthearted novella goes down easy — "I went to look at the girl who is getting married" — and immediately begins to unsettle the gut. Like so many of Matsuda's straightforward sentences, the solidity of the assertion reveals itself to be a false floor. Put your ear to the ground and you'll hear the roar of subterranean worlds, bubbling aquifers of memory.

I often feel with Matsuda's short fiction that I am on a glass-bottom boat, where transparent panels of language reveal ghostly coral reefs and alien shapes in the dark. There is a lovely, scary dissonance between her pellucid prose and those slippery states of being to which her language gives us access.

Consider that verb, "to look at." It scans beautifully. Its weirdness is right at the threshold of detectability. We might easily pass over it, but wait a moment — "to look at"? That's the object of this visit? Huh. OK. So this is not your usual social call. And so we enter twilight territory, the realm of the mysterious mundane.

The girl who is getting married is waiting for us at the top of a coldly luminous staircase that reminds our narrator of a gentle dinosaur. The mix of specific and amorphous details leaves the setting open to interpretation. Yet everything confirms that the girl who is getting married is as precious and as static as a museum piece.

Then a paragraph later, we learn that the narrator has met up with the girl who is getting married "quite recently," at the train station! Moreover, we are assured, "there was not the slightest tension in the smile of the girl who is getting married." This statement, so casually delivered, and so innocent on its surface, immediately provokes our suspicion, springloading the tale with a most delicious tension.

Each new paragraph shifts our understanding of their relationship. At some points they seem to merge into one girl, amoeba-like; at other moments, it's tough to believe that they have ever shared a word. Earlier in life, they drank the same milk *bavarois* and dreamed the same dreams; a page later, the girl who is getting married greets our adult narrator in a flu mask, mouthing something behind the cloth.

I love the way Matsuda stains the looking-glass. "Rectangular windows are always tense." Bicycles are preferable to public transport, where "one has no control". "In the fifteen years that we lived there nothing terrible happened".

Such deceptively matter-of-fact observations, delivered in a neutral, mild tone, begin to shade in the outlines of a wildly idiosyncratic personality. Lulls go off as loudly as alarm bells; they are harbingers of coming storms.

With exquisite control, Matsuda suspends her readers at a midpoint between intimacy and estrangement. Fears and longings that we routinely exile from our waking awareness flood in. Just as physicists must use their creative genius to draw invisible forces into the range of our detection, descending into collapsed gold mines and Arctic caverns in search of subatomic particles, so Matsuda designs story-structures with uncanny acoustics, opening spaces where we can hear the echoing cries of our lost and unborn selves.

Here is a brilliant and daring feat of narrative engineering.

Karen Russell

The Girl Who Is

Getting Married

I went to look at the girl who is getting married.

The girl who is getting married is on the top floor of the building.

I have never been to the building before, but it is on a large street so even I manage to find it quickly.

Its walls are the colour of cocoa. There are even flecks of white, reminiscent of the undissolved powder that sometimes remains on the surface of one's cup. I shall not touch the walls, of course, but if I did I am sure they would feel rough against my palms. All of the windows onto the road are round, with crossed lattices. Generally if one had to say whether round windows or rectangular windows give a softer impression, one would say that round ones do. If asked which are more playful, one would say that round ones are. Rectangular windows are always tense. Without question it is easier to go into a building that has something playful about it than one that does not. I approach the building – wondering if the girl who is getting married is all right, being in such a friendly building.

I step through the entrance. I had a vague impression that the building would be rather old and so it is. It must be what people call Showa Modern. The inside walls are cream-coloured plaster, with the exception of the lower parts, one metre up from the floor, which are painted dark green. There are mailboxes on the wall, with the names of residents written in calligraphy pen. There is a small iron box that I imagine contains a switchboard and a mass of wires. These and everything else attached to the wall are painted the same cream colour as the wall itself. That's good, I think. Attention to detail. An unassuming effort to preserve harmony.

Special mention must be made of the stone staircase that rises up in the centre. It is a very large staircase, with a smooth, pale sheen. Even if it were the case that some other stone was used, I would like to assert quite definitely that this is marble. Although the staircase is flanked by rooms on both sides, its presence is so powerful that there would seem no exaggeration in suggesting that it is the reason for the building's existence. Followed up and up by an obedient black hand-rail, the staircase is an unobtrusive white, a little grey in places, bringing to mind the bones of a dinosaur. I do not know a great deal about dinosaurs so I cannot identify the exact type, but I am thinking of one with a very long neck. One that looks as though it would eat vegetation rather than meat. A comparatively gentle one.

This is a dinosaur that, stretching out its elegant neck, will take me to the room where the girl who is getting married will be.

I met up quite recently with the girl who is getting married. I had not seen the girl who is getting married for a year and when the girl who is getting married appeared at the north entrance of the station I thought how well she looked. The girl who is getting married came through the ticket barrier and when she saw me standing beside the bronze nude statue she smiled, waved and broke into a little run. There was not the slightest tension in the smile of the girl who is getting married. I smiled back, as I always do.

I have known the girl who is getting married since middle school. It goes without saying that in those days she was not the girl who is getting married. We wore the same uniform - a dowdy old blazer and pleated skirt. The girl who is getting married and I were both remarkably slow to achieve enlightenment as to the truths of style. And so the girl who is getting married and I both wore our skirts unfashionably long, without ever realising that they were unfashionably long. We had our lessons in the same class and had lunch at the same time. We were not the type who particularly enjoyed school every day. The feeling that the girl who is getting married and I shared in the classroom was: I don't really know why, but I've got no energy.

I knew her at high school too. Not many of us went on to the same high school so the girl who is getting married and I became even closer. Whenever one of us got a part-time job, the other would then go along and be interviewed as well. It was me that started first at the soba shop by the station, and the girl who is getting married soon joined me. Perhaps in reaction to how she had been at middle school, the girl who is getting married was now a girl who always wears miniskirts. The owner's wife, who ruled the roost, told her not to, but she carried on regardless. The owner's wife had strong likes and dislikes, and inevitably the girl who is getting married incurred her displeasure from a very early stage. And even though I always wore sensible trousers she ended up disliking me too, just because I was a friend of the girl who is getting married. Our next job was at a curry shop the other side of the station. The owner had big goggling eyes and big boastful opinions. There was a rather nervous regular customer there and the owner would mutter about him disdainfully: 'It makes me sad to see someone like that.' I hated it when he said that sort of thing. I thought I was keeping my feelings to myself, but actually it must have shown on my face because the girl who is getting married took the trouble to announce to me one day that 'the boss doesn't like you. Okada-san told me.' Again, we left the job together. Jobs are short-lived during adolescence. But for the girl who is getting married and me they were our first contact with the big wide world. It was very reassuring to have beside me the girl who is getting married, and I hope the girl who is getting married felt the same way having me beside her.

After we left high school we took different paths. The girl who is getting married and I both moved jobs quite a lot, but we still met up two or three times a year. And on one of these occasions, the girl who is getting married announced that she was now a girl who is getting married. The girl who is getting married is getting married! And to be told this in a bar on the way home from work! I felt so grown-up! A few of my work colleagues had got married, but it had never seemed real, their marriages never had anything to do with me. The marriage of the girl who is getting married was different. It had such a vivid reality it was almost as if I was getting married myself. In celebration of my maturity, and of the maturity of the girl who is getting married, I drank eagerly that night. It felt good to be an adult. The girl who is getting married was drinking too. She seemed somewhere along the line to have developed quite a capacity.

In preparation for the wedding this weekend of the girl who is getting married, I have decided to have my hair dyed. Having been brought up at a time when form teachers warned that dyeing one's hair would frazzle one's brains I had never thought of doing it before, so this is my first try. It seems to me that with black hair I cannot express how happy I feel for the girl who is getting married. I have bought a new dress, shoes, and bag for the big day. I thought if I don't buy new things now, then when will I? I want to do everything I can to celebrate. But I am an adult, a burgeoning pillar of society. However happy I feel at the wedding, I shall have to go back to work the next day. A pink afro would lead to complications. I discuss the matter with the stylist and in the end we settle on a slightly cheerful brown. Maybe not that much of a difference to its natural colour, but I think the girl who is getting married will appreciate how I really feel.

My head is all wrapped up. The dye is stinging my scalp but I am coping with the pain. The next chair is occupied by someone whom I am sure nobody would object to me referring to as an old lady. She has just had a perm and now her hair is being dried. A bespectacled young man wields the dryer and her short white hair billows gently in the stream of air. It looks lovely. I gaze at her in the mirror, entranced. How delightful it would be to sleep in that hair! I have been getting more and more white hairs myself recently. At first I had just come across the odd one occasionally and pulled it out. But before long the encounters became more frequent, and now white hairs have begun to sprout in little patches. Discovery of a white patch plunges me into darkness. I would rather go completely white at once, and be like the old lady

next to me. It is beautiful like that. My hair, though, just
looks ugly. Hopeless. How long will I have to wait until my
hair is like hers? I want to be older. I want to grow old at
once, vaulting over this half-baked half-way stage. But now, at
least temporarily, my hair, with all its strands of white, will
be able to hide behind the dye. A slightly cheerful brown will
allow me to forget my white hair problem for a while. It may be
good to live this lie for a little – an unexpected by-product
of the wedding of the girl who is getting married.

The top floor is in fact only the fifth floor. I verified this
on the mailboxes. I wish all buildings in the world were like
this one. I do not like those tall glass buildings that soar
up over city business districts. I always worry that, just as
with the Tower of Babel, God will punish people for building
something so high. And although I certainly had not built it,
and had never expressed any agreement that it should be built,
I would not escape God's punishment. God would not target only
the people who had given the plan the go-ahead. It is terribly
unfair. But nobody would listen if I said I did not want to be
punished for their pride. At best I would be thought odd. So I
keep quiet, even though I think it is wrong.

Are people all right, working so far from the ground? How
do they feel up there, every day? I remember an animated film
about a fine, hard-working boy in a mine. One day a girl wearing
a mysterious pendant comes down from the sky and pleads with
him to leave, saying that people cannot live away from ground
level. I often remember her words when I am in a tall building
or an aeroplane. I regret the folly of having brought myself
to such a dangerous place. And I resent how easily I have been
swayed by others. The film is often shown on television and,
whatever I am doing, I always find myself watching it. It slips
its message in again and again. People cannot live away from
the ground. I am utterly convinced that this is true.

But despite the extreme danger, people have jobs in these
high-rise buildings. They carry on working there day after
day, morning till night. I wonder about their sanity. I could

not do it. I absolutely could not do it. Even if I managed to start working there, cladding my heart in armour, making believe that everything was fine, one day the height of the place would suddenly come home to me. My knees would buckle. I would be unable to move a single step. I can just imagine myself crouching down, unable to look up. My closest colleague, Yumi-chan — we started work on the same day — would look worried. She would take me by the hand and lead me down to the building's main doors. In her other hand would be my briefcase. I would bid farewell forever to the high-rise building and to my pretty high-heeled colleague. *Sayonara!* Our paths will never cross again. An entirely inevitable and utterly ridiculous ending. I always think that in the event of some terrible disaster, I do not want, if at all possible, to be in a place where I cannot cope, where I cannot do anything. But that is hardly realistic if one lives and works in society. In fact, to my intense frustration, there may be nowhere that I can cope, nowhere that I can do anything.

I meet the girl who is getting married five days a week. The girl who is getting married and I registered with different agencies but were sent to the same location. We work on the information desk of a cultural facility that has seen better days. The girl who is getting married and I have the same uniform — a terrible body-hugging dress, yellow-green with black checks, thick starchy synthetic material, horrible to wear. For cold weather there is a short jacket in the same material, but it is too narrow for my shoulders so they get terribly stiff. For the hot summer months we wear short-sleeved dresses. They looked a looser, more comfortable design than the long-sleeved ones, so I thought they would bring some relief, but in fact they have a thick lining sewn into the back, which makes them very hot to wear. It is truly a uniform from hell. The girl who is getting married and I spend more time in the uniform than we do in ordinary clothes, so we complain to each other about it a great deal. The subject is never exhausted.

We stand united in our detestation of our uniform.

Another aspect of our summer dress code is thin tights. I cannot stand them. They are unforgivably hot and itchy, it is true, but what I find quite unbearable is their lack of durability. Things cost money, and costing money, they should last a certain amount of time. That is only reasonable, a matter of common courtesy. But thin tights could not care less. They show no respect whatever for people's sensitivities. In no time at all you have a hole, and then a ladder. The slightest split of a fingernail can bring disaster. As work wear they are completely inappropriate. And on top of this is the constant stress of expenditure. I am supposed to be here to earn money, but I find myself frittering my income away on these incomprehensible tights. The situation is absurd. At first I bought sets of five pairs for five hundred yen, but these had zero durability, often lasting just one outing. They made no financial sense. Three hundred yen a pair is a financial impossibility of course, so now I choose packs of five for one thousand yen. I found them in a drugstore in the next town. They sparkled on the display rack. I use each two-hundred-yen pair for as long as I possibly can. If they fray I daub on nail polish to stop the damage spreading. With wear they grow looser and softer. But inevitably their end comes. Even if by some miracle no holes appear over the visible parts of one's legs, the gusset will eventually give out. It becomes unbelievably thin, as delicate as a spider's web. I gaze at it sometimes as I sit on the lavatory with my tights down. It's amazing it's lasted so long, I think. They've done well, these tights. I can't ask them to do any more. But every time a pair is used up I suffer a two-hundred-yen loss. I keep a constant mental tally. I worry about tights expenditure all through the summer. I long for autumn, when we can wear thicker tights, ones that are far more durable. If I try, I can make one pair of thick tights last all winter.

"Another death," says the girl who is getting married. She has arrived back at the information desk after a patrol of the exhibits.

"What? Another?"

"Yes. May he rest in peace!"

The girl who is getting married and I leave the desk, walk across to the entrance hall, and peer into the fish tank.

Fish have been dying every day. Two weeks ago the man who looks after the tank came and said that if a fish didn't like the new water it might die. It was natural. Oh, we thought. But now we wonder if all this death is really natural. Isn't there too much of it? The contorted body of a fish is floating on the surface of the water.

"Oh! It's the one that was going round and round in circles."

"Yes. It's stopped at last."

One can tell when a fish is going to die. Some develop a kind of fuzziness around their bodies. Some start swimming oddly. Some spend a lot of time floating at an angle, perfectly still. Some have been injured by other fish, perhaps ones that have been rendered vicious by new water. When one sees a fish like that, one can be sure it will be dead the next day. Today's casualty seemed to have been injured around the eye. Anyway, for whatever reason, it had lost its equilibrium and could not swim properly. Instead it went around and around in circles as though it were mad. It was painful to watch and must have seemed very odd to visitors. They had come to enjoy themselves. They had not paid their entrance charge to see a dying fish. I watched them fall silent in front of the tank. To cheer themselves up, they disappeared into other parts of the facility. But there was not much to lift their sprits in any of the other rooms. As staff, we felt extremely apologetic. The dead fish lies sad and thin on the surface of the water. Other fish are nibbling at it.

"The fish world is very cruel!"

"Awful!"

The girl who is getting married and I stared at the dead fish. Even the smallest of deaths has an undeniable splendour when it happens in front of you.

"Shall I get Yamazaki-san?" said the girl who is getting married, snapping out of her reverie.

She walked back towards the reception desk. I followed a short distance behind. She telephoned the office and informed them that another fish had died. Yamazaki would come straight over, roll up his sleeve and take the dead fish away.

The girl who is getting married and I sat down next to each other at the counter. Not many visitors come on a weekday afternoon. Not many come at the weekend either, but even fewer come on weekdays.

The facility opened in a flurry back when the country was at the height of an economic boom that now seems the stuff of fantasy. That bubble burst long ago, and it seems strange that the facility remains. There is very little for us to do. I gaze at people passing by beyond the glass front door, while beside me the girl who is getting married begins gently to rub her thighs and knees. I guess she just wants to keep her hands occupied, but I ask her what she's doing.

"I like stroking my tights. It calms me down," says the girl who is getting married shyly. "It upsets me to look at the water tank."

"I hate thin tights," I said. "I wish they didn't exist."

"Really?" she said. "They make your legs feel so smooth. It's nice!"

The girl who is getting married eases her hands back and forth along her thighs. I had never thought of tights in that way. I touched my thighs. My legs were certainly much smoother than they were without tights. It had never even crossed my mind.

Today I have come to the building by bicycle. It was quite a journey — the equivalent of five stops on the train. But it is my day off, and I did not want to use public transport. It is difficult to escape if there is an emergency on a train or bus. One has no control at all — they move purely by the will of the driver. And I very much doubt that in an emergency passengers would reach consensus on how to act. People have completely different thoughts. It is easy to imagine passengers all behaving in different ways, with very sad results. That is always happening in films. So I do not like to use public transport more than necessary. Most especially I like to avoid the underground. I suppose there was no space left, but these new lines are dug far too deep. If anything happened down there I feel I would get the blame myself. You knew it might happen all along! You shouldn't have come down so far! Coming up so far, coming down so far — it's your own fault!

I often wonder if people are not frightened.

Don't they feel scared?

There is a certain type of people in this world whom I regard as extremely brave. And sometimes, because they are too brave, they seem to be very frightening creatures. Sometimes I suspect that bravery simply means not thinking about anything. Why do they make buildings reach up towards Heaven? It is hopes and dreams that should reach Heaven, not physical things. Do they not feel any disgust at the act of trying to reach the sky with something physical? Wherever I am, I like to have a solid sense of what floor I am on. I never want to forget that when I am on a high floor I am somewhere frightening, somewhere insecure.

The girl who is getting married has done very well. The fifth floor is neither too high nor too low. It is extremely absolutely right. So far there is nothing that I do not like about the girl who is getting married. I just keep on being impressed.

Heading for the fifth floor, I begin to climb the stairs. I move my feet carefully so as not to upset the dinosaur. Normally my back is hunched up a little because of my work, but now it feels perfectly straight.

On the train I sat next to the girl who is getting married. She had a wedding magazine spread out on her lap. At first I was not sitting next to the girl who is getting married,

but to a young man. Affixed to his head were a remarkably
large set of headphones. They suggested classical music, a
splendid home audio room, a lagoon-like sofa and a glass of
wine in one hand. But here he was, absorbed in a game on his
telephone. It may possibly be that he did regard the train
seat as a luxurious sofa, for he sat there as grandly as a
company president, stretching his limbs in all directions –
in other words making life most uncomfortable for me in the
next seat. His flank was flush against me, and as he played the
game his elbow vibrated against the side of my back. I did my
best to show my displeasure, shifting sharply away from him,
staring witheringly down at his game. But this had no effect.
A combination of his headphones and an extremely long fringe
had cut me off entirely. It was a most regrettable situation
– but perhaps I should feel grateful to him. I was already
weakened by an absence of phone messages, and the young man
was helpfully dealing the decisive blow. At the third station
he got off the train. A man in a beige sweatshirt, who had been
standing in front of me, now displayed a desire to occupy the
vacant seat. Showing no consideration to issues of balance
or what might there be to the right or left of the space in
question, he let himself drop onto the seat with a mighty
thud. As expected, his thigh pressed against mine. I made
some extravagant efforts to assert a distance between us, but
no sooner had I contrived to establish the tiniest pocket of
air than it had been absorbed into his zone of pleasure. It
was quite disgraceful. Disgusting. Disgusting to be touching
him, and disgusting to think that my displeasure did not
communicate itself to him at all. He opened up a largely
pornographic 'sports' newspaper. I could not relax. Why on
earth was he sitting with his legs splayed out like that? What
are muscles for after all? And still I had no messages. Not a
bleep, not a shiver from my bag. I sat forward, perching on the
edge of my seat in an effort to avoid eye contact. But then I
changed tack. I fixed my eyes on him and made a show of rising
to my feet. He looked back in surprise. I hope that at least
some of my disgust was conveyed. I moved forward into the next

carriage. And there I found the girl who is getting married.

It was pleasant to be next to the girl who is getting married. She did not sit with her legs apart. She did not infringe on my space. There was a comfortable distance between us. What a relief! The wedding magazine was open on her lap. I sat back in my seat and peered past her shoulder towards the pages. Its cloud of pink and white floated up towards my eyes – there seemed nothing to focus on. Do you really want that? I silently asked the girl who is getting married. It is so much more pleasant sitting with another woman like this. Do you really want that? The bag on my lap shook. I put my hand inside and brought out my phone. There was a message. I checked it quickly. It was from a friend. That does not count. This message is not a message. I have not had a message all week. I put the phone back in my bag without replying. The girl who is getting married was still avidly reading her bulky magazine, sticking labels to parts of particular interest. The girl who is getting married had her pink labels clasped in her left hand. It is more pleasant to sit with another woman, so why am I waiting for a message? Still waiting for messages at my age! Perhaps the girl who is getting married does not have to bother any more about waiting for messages. Perhaps she can relax simply turning the pages of her pink and white magazine. Just that was enough to make me feel I was jealous.

I climb the stairs one by one, and I wonder: What expression is on the face of the girl who is getting married as she sits in her room? Is she thinking, Oh, the fifth floor is so relaxing! The fifth floor is such a good height! If so, I think the girl who is getting married and I are going to get on well. But then perhaps she is thinking, Oh, it's such a pain having to walk up all these stairs every day. If only there was an elevator! It is certainly true that it is not common these days to find a five-storey building without an elevator. I reach the third floor and am beginning to be short of breath. But this is the charm of the building. And in fact I am relieved

there is no elevator. I loathe elevators. Nothing is worse
than being shut up inside one of those iron boxes even for
a few seconds. And the boxes go up and down! I cannot get
used to that movement, especially down. However much I steel
myself, I feel sick in the pit of my stomach. I cannot imagine
how people can want to bungee jump or go on those free-fall
attractions at amusement parks. And then sometimes one finds
oneself alone in an elevator with a man. I do not like that
at all. What if the elevator stops and I am stuck inside with
him? What if he starts behaving oddly? It worries me stupid.
For a coward like me it is much nicer to have no elevator at
all. With a staircase all I have to do is calmly walk step by
step up a prepared route — like the yellow brick road in *The
Wizard of Oz*. There is absolutely nothing unsettling about
a staircase. You are not shut in. You are not sent hurtling
downwards at an outrageous speed. If anything happens, you can
run down the stairs. I hope the girl who is getting married
will run down the stairs, gamely, at her own pace. I look out
of the window on the landing. I see the large shopping mall
that has been built in the next town. They are promoting it as
'a multi-purpose amusement park'. Besides all its shops there
is a game centre for children and a bowling alley, as well as a
cinema right next door. I have been there once. It is so bright
you could forget the human race has such a thing as shadows.
Cheerful music plays nonstop through speakers you cannot see,
but must be somewhere. All these shops, but not a single one I
like, not a single thing I want. It is strange. With children's
high-pitched voices reverberating from the tall domed ceiling,
I went into the hellish food court and had a fresh-squeezed
orange juice before going home. It was delicious.

I was in the same group as the girl who is getting married,
but I never knew the girl who is getting married was the girl
who is getting married. The girl who is getting married was
next to me, chopping spring onions. She was very good with
her hands. First we sat around the worktop at the front
and listened to the teacher. Apparently, the teacher was a

prominent figure in the cookery world and had written several
books. The cookery school was in a building I passed on the
way home from work. They had had some cancellations so were
accepting students immediately before the class. It sounded
fun so I thought I would give it a try. The girl who is getting
married was a fan of this particular chef and had eagerly
applied for the class at a very early stage. She had one of
the chef's books in her bag and wanted to get it signed if the
chance arose. Once the teacher's introduction was over we were
split arbitrarily into groups of four and assigned to different
worktops. Each worktop was stocked with appropriate amounts
of the basic ingredients and very finely measured quantities
of seasoning. The seasoning containers had had their labels
removed so that the brand could not be identified. Besides the
girl who is getting married and me, the other two in our group
seemed to be friends and laughed together as they embarked on
the task. The girl who is getting married was not the type to
start talking freely with people she did not know. She followed
the recipe silently from the print-out we had been given,
thinking back to the demonstration the chef had just given us.
The knife and spring onions struck a good rhythm.   It was a
beginners' class designed for people who could spare a little
time on their way home at the end of the day, so the cooking
task was soon finished. We were making Japanese-style omelettes
and mushroom soup, a very simple menu, I thought, but even
so the excitement of the beginners, the true participants in
the course, was infectious, at least for me. Having quietly
brought their own completed dishes to the table, everybody
produced phones and cameras from their bags and started
taking pictures, as though that was the whole purpose of the
evening. I suppose the pictures were destined for blogs and
so on. Not content with their own and classmates' work, some
were photographing the chef's examples at the front of the
classroom, undeterred by the fact that the food could hardly
be seen through the condensation on the plastic wrap. They
all wanted to capture them, to keep them. In the tumult the

girl who is getting married took out her phone, took a single photograph of the dishes she had made and then began to eat. *I guessed that the girl who is getting married would also be putting the photo on a blog. But in fact the girl who is getting married did not have a blog. The photograph was sent to her fiancé on the train home. But of course, without notification by her or somebody else, one could not have told at a glance that she was the girl who is getting married.

The fourth floor. Soon I shall be getting to the girl who is getting married. The girl who is getting married is quite unaware that I am coming. I imagine her opening the window for some fresh air, filling her lungs, gazing out at the familiar landscape, feeding breadcrumbs to the birds that have come to her balcony. What a beautiful view there is from the fifth floor! It is quite perfect. Any further up or down would be too much or too little. Further up and you have the creeping fear of height. Further down is too close to the turbulence of the world. The reason I know so much about the fifth floor, the reason I am so fond of it, is that I am, I tell you quite frankly, a girl who was brought up on the fifth floor.

When I was a child the family lived in an eight-storey block. Our flat was on the fifth floor. It is doubtless largely on account of the size of that building of my childhood that today my upper tolerance level is set at eight floors. Nine may just about be manageable, but once we are into double digits there is no hope. I shrivel inside. I curl up like an armadillo. My needles stick out like a hedgehog's.

In the fifteen years that we lived there nothing terrible happened, either to us or to the other people in the block. Well, I suppose there were problems for individual families: husbands being unfaithful; children struggling to get into good universities; cats that had to be hidden from the caretaker and consequent panic every time the doorbell rang. But there were no major problems relating to the building itself. The worst incident was probably when residents from the two floors above presented a complaint to the building management committee about the smell from a food outlet at ground level.

There were two business tenants at ground level. The one on the left was originally a café called Marronnier run by Mrs Okudaira, a lady from the fourth floor.

In Marronnier there was a sad-looking ceramic-faced doll. The lavatory doorknobs were covered with flower-patterned kilt fabric, lacy around the edges. Coffee was served in richly patterned Imari ware, Indian tea in pretty, bright Liberty-print cups and saucers. Mrs Okudaira had patiently collected a variety of different cups through the years. One of the secret joys for housewives visiting Marronnier was wondering which they would get. It was a peaceful place, free of stress. If a child came home from school to find their door locked and nobody about, they would pause only for a moment before thinking "Oh she must be down there!" Then they would run down the stairs to Marronnier, fling open the door, and mother and child would be reunited.

Mrs Okudaira had a curly brown perm, and immaculate makeup around her eyes. She would glide gracefully around the café, fielding local gossip and family chat from the succession of housewives who drifted in. As I sat with a comic book under the living arch of conversation woven by my mother and her friends, Mrs Okudaira's hand would slip in unobtrusively and place in front of me a cork coaster and a cream soda.

The food outlet opened when this housewife oasis closed. The Okudairas moved away one day and the new place was run by outsiders. Perhaps when Mrs Mimura from 2.04 and Mrs Okada from 3.05 complained at the management meeting about the new shop, it was not really the smell that bothered them. Perhaps what they really wanted was to mark Marronnier's disappearance – a lost café, a lost time. Eventually, our family left the block too. Now I live alone. And other members of the family live their separate lives.

I had completely forgotten about Marronnier. It has all been

brought back to me by the building of the girl who is getting
married. C'est la vie. I wonder if the girl who is getting
married has evenings when she stares into the distance and
thinks how far she has wandered. I do. Too often. But of course
the girl who is getting married must be happier than I am.
After all, the girl who is getting married is getting married.

I pluck a hair from the skin of the girl who is getting
married. It must be the third time the girl who is getting
married has come to this salon where I work as a hair removal
specialist. They say that laser is the most usual method these
days, but this place specialises in electric removal, a one-
hair-at-a-time method that suits me very well. I have always
had an almost pathological affection for detail. The idea of a
laser removing hairs simultaneously over a large area of skin
gives me indigestion. Most of my clients are women. On their
first visit I explain about the hair growth cycle and hair
loss. Then they lie down on the treatment table and I start
removing hairs in the requested area. The process involves
a slight electric current, so their bodies stiffen when the
needle is inserted. And during the actual hair removal they do
experience a certain amount of pain. Nevertheless, we have a
constant flow of clients. Of course we do. All they have to do
is endure pain and that will be the end of their lonely battle
against hair. How much time have they spent on hair so far?
Add it all up and hair removal has probably taken each of them
at least one long weekend. Sheer waste! And why anyway are we
supposed to think that something which grows naturally is not
normal, that we are more beautiful without it? Who decided this
and when? Ever since adolescence I have thought it very odd.
But I still kept on plucking and shaving, and of course the
hairs quickly grew back again. This was going to carry on until
I died. The mere thought made me feel faint. Yet before long
I had become obsessed with plucking. It was an addiction —
the feel of hair coming out from the root as I pulled the
tweezers, the gradual expansion of the hairless territory. The
same impulse made me love weeding too.

And destiny has somehow kept me plucking. Most of my colleagues are now younger than I am. If you spend each day plucking hairs, it gets to feel ridiculous sometimes. But I still find the work exciting. My eyesight is weakening, but I am still good at it. I always chat away to the women while I pluck. It keeps their minds off the pain. And it was while chatting that I learnt that the girl who is getting married is the girl who is getting married.

The girl who is getting married was a careful planner. Once it had been decided that the girl who is getting married is getting married next year, she started going to a hair removal salon in order that she could wear a wedding dress with a bare back and shoulders. To deal with her breadth of back she went to a laser salon, and at the same time, in the same salon, started armpit treatment. When the density of hair had been substantially reduced, she came to complete the treatment at the salon where I work. The girl who is getting married explained all this to me as she lay on the treatment table, one arm above her head like a backstroke swimmer. For this once-in-a-lifetime wedding the girl who is getting married will leave nothing to chance. The girl who is getting married eagerly describes how fussy she is, how detailed her plans are. Last month she went all the way to France to choose her wedding dress. She has an energy I do not have. And money. The girl who is getting married and I speak once every month or two. The girl who is getting married is trying to make a dream wedding reality. She went to Kyoto last week to order special *konpeito* confectionery to hand out to her guests. How feeble she makes me feel! If I had the drive of the girl who is getting married I would not be in a place like this endlessly picking out hairs. But for me it is all right. Meanwhile, the girl who is getting married is getting to the end of her underarm hair removal programme.

As with the other floors, the fifth has the staircase in the middle, with rooms on either side. I understand that the girl

who is getting married is in the one on the right. I am now
on the same floor as the girl who is getting married. In other
words, I am at the same height as the girl who is getting
married. I stand for a while outside the door of the room
where the girl who is getting married is expected to be. The
only thing separating me and the girl who is getting married
is a cream-colour-painted steel door. I pressed the intercom
buzzer of the girl who is getting married. I heard someone
on the other side of the door, footsteps came closer. A heavy
clunk, and the door opened. The girl who is getting married
appeared. Our eyes met.

To my surprise the girl who is getting married was wearing
a flu mask. With her nose and mouth covered by the mask, it
is difficult to get a clear picture of her face overall. I
noticed a widening of her eyes from which I surmised that
the girl who is getting married was surprised by my sudden
visit. The girl who is getting married gazed at me for a while
with uncertainty. It may have been that she was trying to
communicate something just by moving her lips, but I am afraid
that since the girl who is getting married was wearing a flu
mask, even if I had known how to lip-read it would have been no
help. We stared at each other.

The girl who is getting married is in the room. She has a
cushion on her lap and is watching television. The girl who
is getting married is two years older than I am. I have spent
more time with the girl who is getting married than I have
with anybody else in my life. The family album is full of
photographs of us playing around together — like two little
bears. The girl who is getting married and I have engaged
each other in many fierce struggles, both physical and mental.
I have not forgotten how when I was at kindergarten the girl
who is getting married picked up a stick on the road and hit
me with it. The girl who is getting married bears a scar on
the sole of her foot from a pencil lead that I dropped and
could not be bothered to pick up. After years of invasion and
compromise, ignoring and being ignored, just when we had grown

to understand each other's sense of distance and had achieved a stable relationship, the girl who is getting married became the girl who is getting married.

The voice of the girl who is getting married grew sweeter after she became the girl who is getting married. Perhaps it sounded entirely the same to everyone else, but I knew the difference. Her voice was as sweet as the milk *bavarois* that rests deep inside me.

When I was small, my mother would make us treats on Sundays. It was a good effort on her part — she was a rather impatient person and not that keen on household tasks. She made quite a variety of things: shaped cookies, yoghurt cakes, orange caramel pudding, and so on, and amongst them was milk bavarois She mixed finely chopped strawberries and kiwi fruit together with milk, gelatine, fresh cream, and sugar. Any sugar that did not dissolve would sink to the bottom of the bowl. So when the *bavarois* had set and was turned out onto a plate for us to eat, the un-dissolved sugar would be on top. We crunched it between our jaws, filling our mouths with intoxicating sweetness. Whenever the girl who is getting married and I ate my mother's milk *bavarois*, we would feel bewitched. We would be in a dream. Sunday afternoon would gradually change colour, from faintly browning lemon juice to amber. I remember the slim legs of the girl who is getting married sprawled to one side. I was like a honey bee caught in amber, a child who knew nothing of past or future. I never sensed the future, never felt anxious about what might happen to me. It must have been the same for the girl who is getting married. She was always next to me, always facing the same direction, looking vacant. We just kept standing there, stock still, hand in hand.

The voice of the girl who is getting married seemed to carry happy memories, like that of the milk *bavarois*. I wonder if the girl who is getting married still remembers its sweetness. Has the girl who is getting married thought how many memories we share? Will the girl who is getting married get married with that sweetness inside her? Will she have children and make sweet things for them? But the sweet memory of *bavarois* is in my body too. What is the difference? A girl who is getting married and a girl who is not getting married – what does it matter? I sometimes wish someone would tell me that my voice is sweet, the voice of me as I am now.

It is a long time since I last saw her so it is a shame that the face of the girl who is getting married is almost entirely hidden by her flu mask. I would not deny being biased, but the girl who is getting married has a very lovely face. Considering the time of year, I suppose that the girl who is getting married has hay fever. This is strange. A girl who is getting married having hay fever. Should not a girl who is getting married radiate such happiness that any pollen would scuttle away, its tail between its legs? A girl who is getting married wearing a flu mask?

I have attended several weddings in my life but I have never seen a bride with hay fever. I have never seen a bride wearing a flu mask, nor, of course, walking around with pocket tissues. Wedding dresses do not have pockets – which goes to show that brides with hay fever have never been considered a possibility. I suppose if one wore Japanese-style wedding clothes one could hide a tissue up one's sleeve, but I have never seen such a thing - I have never seen a bride taking a tissue from her kimono sleeve.

No, it is truly astonishing that the girl who is getting married should be suffering because of pollen. I thought a girl who is getting married repels evil things. She is protected by magic. She is the strongest creature in the world. Once she is engaged, right through the wedding and honeymoon no problem can occur. It is only after she returns to ordinary life that the magic gradually wears off. The very idea that she could be hit by something like hay fever!

First of all, before I forgot, I thought I would give back to the girl who is getting married the money I owed her. But she refused. It was not a large amount – about four hundred

yen. We were planning to have supper at my house and had gone
shopping at the nearby supermarket. I did not have change on
me, so the girl who is getting married gave me what she had.
She lent me it immediately. Her timing showed she had been
watching what I was doing. That sort of thing happens quite
often, and sometimes our roles are reversed. We gradually
stop noticing these little loans. We begin to share things
more and more; distinctions that were clear-cut become vague.
And now the girl who is getting married and I are getting
married. Marriage is the natural evolution of our relationship.
Our separate outlines will blur; more and more things will
become ambiguous. It will be as though the two of us have just
one mind. I think it is a wonderful thing to happen. But on
the other hand I suppose there are some phenomena that will
suddenly reveal themselves in stark outline.

We have finished supper. The girl who is getting married is
washing the dishes and I am wiping the table. I have never
been able to think of wiping the table or washing the dishes
as 'housework'. What is meant by the word 'housework'? Is
it right to give things like washing and cooking – things
that are obviously necessary parts of life – a name like
'housework'? Does it not make them suddenly sound like a duty?
I live on my own and I have never been conscious of anything
like that being 'housework'. I have always just done it. I
think it is the same for the girl who is getting married. But
when different people end up living in the same house, suddenly
these acts all become 'housework'. They are suddenly on parade
in front of you, solid and serious. At that moment you have
to start thinking about sharing responsibilities, about
workloads. After a while one side will begin to feel aggrieved,
thinking they are doing more than the other. This will result
in a quarrel. And the quarrel will tire both sides out. Is that
reasonable? If you do not get married, then the act of washing
dishes is simply the act of washing dishes. I do not want to
turn the act of washing dishes into 'housework'. How far can
we get without making washing dishes 'housework'? But then

it is because I think we can manage it that I want to marry the
girl who is getting married. That is the kind of thing that has
been running through my mind recently. The girl who is getting
married is cheerfully washing the dishes at the moment, but I am
frightened of the day I see her tired of life. It may be that I
am the reason why the girl who is getting married is tired. That
frightens me. That's what he says. What does that matter? I say.
We can deal with it when it happens. That's what I think, but men
can be so sensitive sometimes, can't they? It's odd, says the girl
who is getting married. She has been on the telephone for half an
hour complaining about her fiancé. Because of my position young
people often ask me for advice. I do not mind, but the truth is I
simply do not know what to say. Well, yes, I mutter. I suppose so.
No, well, uh-huh.

The girl who is getting married invited me in. The room was
very tidy. There is a small wooden bookcase against the wall,
on top of which is a silver photograph frame that I gave to the
girl who is getting married. In the frame is a photograph of
the girl who is getting married and me. We are smiling. It takes
me back. I am happy that she has displayed it. I sit down on a
chair by the dining table while the girl who is getting married
makes tea. I gazed at the side of her masked face. I began to
worry about the girl who is getting married. Of course I have
been always thinking about her at a distance, but I did not think
that at our ages we should be constantly in touch. So I decided
not to contact her unless she contacted me. But perhaps this has
backfired. The girl who is getting married often caught colds,
often felt unwell. I should have been there for her.
The girl who is getting married brings over a tray with a
glass teapot, two matching cups and two plates with pieces of
the cheesecake I bought on the way here. The girl who is getting
married likes cheesecake. I am feeling relieved —relieved that
the girl who is getting married is using an expensive-looking
teapot and elegant foreign crockery, relieved that she is not
using a cheap ceramic pot from a hundred-yen shop, the type you
would feel like smashing to pieces on an evening when nothing had

gone well, relieved that there are herbs sunk to the bottom of her expensive glass pot. I think that this bit of affluence will be a deterrent, will help the girl who is getting married. Help her in life. I do not just mean financially. Something else. I cannot really explain.

I first met the girl who is getting married when I came to university. The snow is deep where I was brought up and I headed east wearing long boots. When I got off the train I was surprised that nobody else was wearing long boots. They suddenly began to feel large and loose. I tramped along the tarmac towards the dormitory where I was going to live. The girls' dormitory was in one corner of the large university campus. It was old and in bad condition. But everything felt fresh to me. I shared a room with the girl who is getting married. The girl who is getting married and I were both from the provinces, and we got on well right from the start. Our life together was in a tatami-matted room of about ten square metres with no lock on the door. There were no beds; we spread out our futon at night and folded them away into the cupboard in the morning. Every morning and evening there was roll-call. We would slide open the wooden door and kneel formally on the floor, waiting for the head of the dormitory to come around. Occasionally one of us would buy some reduced-price flowers at a florist nearby and put them by the window. The petals would be slightly brown around the edges, but the flowers were still pretty. One night before going to bed the girl who is getting married told me that after graduation she was getting married I was surprised. It was the first time marriage had felt so close. Since then I have come across a lot of girls who are getting married. In the end I never became a girl who is getting married, but even so I have a girl who is getting married.

The girl who is getting married poured tea into the cups and put a cup in front of me. She took off the flu mask so that

she could drink from her cup. It had been a long time since I
had seen the face of the girl who is getting married.

"I was surprised when you suddenly turned up. I'd have come
out to meet you if you'd told me."

It had been a long time since I had heard the voice of
the girl who is getting married. The voice of the girl who is
getting married grows kinder with the years. When she was a
little child it was so lovely I wanted to record everything
she said, but for a time in her teens and twenties her voice
was like steel. Meeting her again now, the voice of the girl
who is getting married somehow seemed kinder than ever before.
For a moment it struck me as similar to my sister's voice long
ago. But that thought quickly passed. My sister raised three
children. In the process her thin arms grew thick and strong
and so did her voice. Her arms could hold anything, her voice
reach any distance.

"You didn't have to come here and walk up all those stairs.
We could have met somewhere outside. Your legs are still bad,
aren't they?"

"It's no problem at all. Why are you wearing a flu mask? You
must take care of yourself."

"This?" smiled the girl who is getting married. "There's no
auto-lock on the door. There's a peep-hole, but you can't see
much through it. I feel frightened sometimes so I put on the
mask before opening the door. It's a kind of defence."

What was she trying to defend with it? I suppose a mask
meant the other person could not see her face, but she
certainly seemed to be overestimating its usefulness. I was
not sure whether to see her as steady and reliable, or
just rather hopeless. She had certainly always been amusing.
I sighed to myself. Anyway, tea tastes good on the fifth floor.
It hits the spot.

"I'm going to have a look at the venue today."

"The wedding venue? Take a proper look, won't you. Don't
just wander around like you used to."

That is what Mother might have said. Yes, that is exactly
the sort of thing. I can just imagine. Amused at this thought,

the woman stood up and took her cup to the sink. The other cup
is still in front of the photograph frame. I'll leave it there
till I get back, thinks the woman. In the frame is a faded
photograph. It shows a little girl and a woman in her twenties
or thirties. They are huddled together under a clear winter
sky, smiling at the camera. They look very happy. The girl is
fully rigged out in a woolly hat, thick top, corduroy skirt,
gloves, woollen tights — no skin showing except her face. When
she was small, her tights itched; she hated heavy clothes.
Much later she realised that the woman was setting a boundary
to protect her from the outside world. And now she knows what
that boundary is called. The weather is good today, just like
in the photograph. The petals of the flowers in the vase beside
the frame are browning slightly. I'll go to the florist on the
way back and buy some fresh ones, thinks the woman. She heard
the chirrup of a bird on the balcony and looked outside. She
cannot see a bird, though. Her eyes rest on the streets of
housing stretching out in front of the building. She used to
be able to see the shopping mall in the next town but business
had not been good and it had been demolished some time ago.
It was still a vacant space. She had been looking forward to
seeing what they would build there next, but now she would
probably have moved before she found out. Having completed her
preparations, she went to the hallway and put on her shoes.
As she opened the door, she turned and looked back once more
into the room. Then she went out. Inside the empty room there
was the muffled sound of the door being locked.

About the Project

Keshiki is a series of chapbooks showcasing the work of some of the most exciting writers working in Japan today, published by Strangers Press, part of the UEA Publishing Project.

Each story is beautifully translated and presented as an individual chapbook, with a design inspired by the text.

Keshiki is a unique collaboration between University of East Anglia, Norwich University of the Arts, and Writers' Centre Norwich, funded by the Nippon Foundation.

Supported by

THE NIPPON
FOUNDATION

WRITERS'
CENTRE
NORWICH

University of East Anglia

NORWICH
UNIVERSITY
OF THE ARTS

1 —
Time Differences
Yoko Tawada
Translated by Jeffrey Angles

2 —
Friendship for Grown-Ups
Nao-Cola Yamazaki
Translated by Polly Barton

3 —
Spring Sleepers
Kyoko Yoshida
Translated by Polly Barton

4 —
Mariko/Mariquita
Natsuki Ikezawa
Translated by Alfred Birnbaum

5 —
The Girl Who Is Getting Married
Aoko Matsuda
Translated by Angus Turvill

6 —
At the Edge of the Wood
Masatsugu Ono
Translated by Juliet Winters Carpenter

7 —
Mikumari
Misumi Kubo
Translated by Polly Barton

8 —
The Transparent Labyrinth
Keiichirō Hirano
Translated by Kerim Yasar